WARNING

This book contains adult language and violence. It may be considered offensive to some readers. This book is for sale to adults ONLY.

* * * * * * * * * * * * * * * * *

Please store your files wisely where they cannot be accessed by underage readers.

ISBN-13: 978-1773500768
ISBN-10: 1773500767

Other Books by Freddie Kim:

The Time Guardian Thriller Series

When the Time Guardian goes missing, it is up to Sonia to travel back to the past the rectify the future of humanity. Follow this epic tale of good versus evil in the battle to control Earth's destiny.

Stinger Jacked

The Free Humanity Movement (FHM) resistance hatches a plan to steal a Stinger Class assault ship from OmniClon Universal (OCU) and its alliance partner, the ka'Thar. With morale at an all-time low, Rogal and his team of misfits are sent on what could potentially be a suicide mission.

Get the latest update on new releases from the author at:

https://www.freddiekim.com/newsletter/

This book is Part Two of the "The Cyber Heist Files"

Book 1 – Cyber Heist

The entire financial industry of the World Government is at risk when a weaponized virus is covertly uploaded into the computer system. Faced with an imminent crisis, the government releases the whistle blower, Tyler Wilkens, in exchange for eradicating the virus that has infected their computer systems. Something malevolent is afoot and Wilkens is the best chance the government has to combat it.

Book 2 – Kill Code

When Tyler Wilkens fails to completely eradicate the virus, he is put back in prison and his competitor, another tech company, is tasked with finishing the job. As circumstances turn dire, Wilkens is released once again to do the government's bidding. But what he finds within the computer system is something ominous and unexpected. Will Wilkens be able to save the World Government from complete financial collapse?

Book 3 – Coup D'état

With the World Government ousted in the coup d'état, OmniClon Universal (OCU) attempts to take control over the world. Tasked with finding evidence to save the former government, Wilkens falls deep down the rabbit hole. With the help of Monica Franchette, Wilkens uncovers a conspiracy that leads him to multiple assassinations and the highest levels of authority. The burden of truth does not come without its risks. Will Wilkens be a marked man with a target on his back for the rest of his life?

The Cyber Heist Files

Kill Code

Book Two

By Freddie Kim

Copyright Revelry Publishing 2020

Table of Contents

Chapter One

VICTOR NUGENT and Tyler Wilkens just stood there, astonished, while Clarence Rainer made the urgent call to the President's office.

The tech team had discovered a massive viral infestation within the World Government's financial sector computer systems. The President's office startled them even more by granting them Carte Blanche to deal with the situation. With a massive government payment due within the week, they weren't taking any chances.

"Hold on," said Wilkens. He approached one of the viral blobs. It reacted to his touch. Using his virtual hands, Wilkens picked up the quivering mass. It felt oozy in his hands, like a mass of gelatin. Swiping his hand from left to right, a virtual window popped up. He selected the magnifying glass function, and the image of the blob zoomed up on the screen. He examined it from all angles. But when he looked underneath the blob, there appeared a circular greenish glow. It was pulsating.

"Now this is interesting," said Wilkens excitedly. "I didn't expect this."

"What do you see?" asked Victor, confused.

"I configured my rendering software to pick out certain code fragments that I've identified in my programming sequences," said Wilkens. "See that pulsating green glow underneath this virus?"

Both men uttered at the same time, "Uh huh."

"Well, that's the kill code that I put in my programming," said Wilkens. "It's no secret that hackers and certain programmers will put secret backdoors or kill switches into their programs. I put in a kill-switch fragment in my coding. Only I know about it. Anyone mimicking or trying to build other viruses, even weaponized ones, will end up incorporating a kill code that renders the virus inert."

"What does that mean for us?" asked Clarence.

"Watch this," said Wilkens. He opened the virtual utility folder and pulled out an eyedropper which he placed onto the glowing pulsating greenish glow. He squeezed the bulbous part of the dropper and suctioned up some of the glowing essence. He activated another folder, pulled out a device, and inserted the dropper.

The device had a numerical keypad with selection display. Wilkens scrolled down the selection bar and highlighted Dispersion Grenade. He set the numerical counter at 1,000. Then he pressed the <RUN> button. In a matter of moments, dispersion grenades started popping out of the device.

"This is it. Everybody, pick up as many grenades as you can handle and put them into your rucksacks. I'll show you how to use them," said Wilkens.

After the device finished producing the full number of grenades and they were packed away, Wilkens and the group moved on to each virus-infected virtual corridor. He plucked a grenade out of his rucksack and pulled the pin.

"Although we're in a virtual environment, you should plug your ears and take shelter. You'll have only a few seconds to find cover once you launch," said Wilkens.

"Do as I do when we're in the vicinity of these viruses," said Wilkens. He tossed the activated grenade into the center of the infected corridor.

The team ducked around the hallway from the main corridor where the grenade was dropped. A split second later, a boom sounded, and they felt the virtual chamber shudder. Wilkens peeked around the wall to assess the damage. He signaled for the others to join him.

"The coast is clear. It's safe to come out," said Wilkens.

The group emerged back onto the corridor, but now all they saw was the red goo of the destroyed viruses throughout the corridor. They were annihilated. The gooey mass was fast turning into red dust, falling and disintegrating into nothing. The corridor was completely clear of the virus.

"Now all we have to do is proceed throughout the financial section of this computer system to clear the entire mess of viruses there. With the three of us, we should be able to rid the system of the virus in a matter of hours."

Chapter Two

"Daddy, can we go to the zoo today?" Sterling was excited to be finally spending a full day with her father.

Although Tyler Wilkens' incarceration had wreaked havoc on his marriage, his ex-wife ensured their daughter's relationship with her father was maintained. After all, he was still considered a hero to many people for his role in exposing government corruption.

The revealing of a network of spy satellites run by a secret state-sponsored agency and used to access the private lives of every citizen should have shocked the world. But instead of admitting to the embarrassment, corrupt government officials had rushed through a piece of legislation that retroactively made their questionable activities legal. Wilkens was charged and convicted of treason, earning him a permanent spot in the penal system.

But now he was free, and he needed to make it up to his daughter for all the years he had been gone.

"Yes, Pumpkin. But is that all you want? I missed your thirteenth birthday last month so you can ask for anything else. I can afford it now." Wilkens smiled at his daughter before turning his head to hide his tearing eyes.

Sterling looked at her father and cautiously asked, "Will you come to my recital? I'm playing in the school talent show."

"Nothing can keep me away. I'm so proud of you," said Wilkens, his heart filled with joy at his daughter's request.

Sterling hopped up and down with excitement, a big smile spanned from ear to ear. "Yes, I can't wait to play for you. It's a surprise." She ran up to her father and jumped into his arms.

He picked her up and gave her a big loving hug. "I wouldn't miss it for the world." But his words were uttered too soon.

As if on cue, an ominous presence seemed to hear his thoughts, and Wilkens heard a commotion at the entrance to his suite. The Assistant Attorney General, Felix Switzer, and six-suited thugs entered the room.

"Go away, guys. I'm retired now," said Wilkens with a hint of hostility. "Can't you see I'm with my daughter?" He didn't even bother to look at who was there, he was so irritated.

"Enjoy the last few minutes of your freedom, Wilkens," said Switzer with disgust. "The government doesn't like traitors who renege on their deals."

"Daddy, those men are scaring me." Sterling anxiously held on tight to her father and buried her head in his chest.

"Honey, don't let these bad men scare you. Now run along and call your mother." Wilkens released his daughter and watched her leave the room before reacting to Switzer's verbal assault. Wilkens raised his head and angrily looked at the men. "What the hell are you talking about?"

Switzer stood with arms crossed, toe tapping the ground, and cold eyes staring at Wilkens. The six thugs formed a threatening circle around Wilkens.

Chapter Three

One Day Earlier

The World Government machine had hummed along proficiently over the last three days, having recovered from part of its computer system crashing, particularly in the financial sector. The accountants and assistants made the final preparations for payments covering various contract services and debts. They also compiled the supporting documents that were due within the next two days. The schedules were set and the automatic payments ready for disbursement. No errant issues were found or anticipated.

Claire, the clerk who oversaw the entire Division of Finance, only noticed an anomaly when she did a routine audit of the payment accounts. She couldn't believe what her screen displayed, so she refreshed the system. After the refresh, the information still seemed incorrect. Perplexed, Claire initiated a full system reboot. Still nothing. Now she was worried. The system showed insufficient funds to cover outstanding payments pending over the next forty-eight hours.

As per protocol, she escalated the issue to her boss. She sent the requisite urgent email, but given the critical nature of the problem, she also sought verbal confirmation that the information was received, so she left her desk and went to the supervisor's office.

"Ms. Welles, I just sent you an email. I think you should look at it," said Claire.

Josie Welles looked up from her screen. She was just going over the divisional status reports for the week. There were many to pore over, but it was routine for her. "Can it wait? I need to finish reviewing the status reports before the manager's meeting in about an hour."

"I don't believe it can wait. I noticed a problem with the system payouts, and I think you should review it now before it gets buried," said Claire.

"You are such an alarmist," sneered Welles as she swore under her breath. This was not the first time her underling had cried wolf. There was always some disaster waiting around the corner, rain behind every cloud.

"You sent me an email, right?" asked Welles.

"Yes, I flagged it as urgent," said Claire.

"So, you did your job. Now get back to work," commanded Welles critically. She was skeptical but decided she would take a look at it after the manager's meeting.

Welles gasped in fury.

"What the hell!" she exclaimed. "Claire, get your ass in here. Right now."

Claire rushed to the door of Welles' office, terrified of her supervisor's anger. But she had given Welles fair warning. "You called?" asked Claire, trying to hide her anxiousness.

"Is this right?" asked Welles. "How could there not be funds in any of our accounts?"

"Your guess is as good as mine. I tried to warn you earlier," said Claire with more confidence, having approached the situation proactively.

Welles was definitely annoyed now. Claire's tendency to cry wolf had put her division in jeopardy. If anyone else had gone to Welles about the issue, she would have considered it immediately. But because it was Claire, Welles assumed it was an exaggerated reaction and she had taken her time to look at the issue just to punish the messenger. Now, it seemed Claire had been right, and Welles was looking bad. Claire's future in her division wasn't looking good; there would be retribution.

"We need to sort this out," said Welles. Feeling overwhelmed and fearing for her job after dropping the ball, she picked up her phone and dialed Saul's extension.

Chapter Four

Not for the first time, Wilkens found himself in the interrogation room. He was not allowed to communicate with anyone outside of the investigation, and restroom privileges were withheld. Ironically, he was allowed to drink as much coffee as he wanted. Now he really had to go.

An agent entered the room.

"I need to go to the restroom. Like right now," said Wilkens.

"In a moment. I just have a few questions for you," said the agent nonchalantly. "By the way, my name is Agent Hansen."

"I told the other guy everything I know," said Wilkens. "If you tell me what you're looking for, maybe I can help you and then go to the damn restroom."

Hansen took his time taking the seat across the table from Wilkens. He slowly removed his dark glasses and placed them in his pocket. "Tell me about this virus in the system."

"I can't tell you what I don't know. You guys won't let me anywhere near the computer system," said Wilkens with disgust.

"The deal was you were supposed to fix the system. Now we have an even bigger problem," said Hansen disapprovingly.

"If you can give me access to a terminal right now, I'll see what I can do. That is, right after I visit the little boy's room," Wilkens offered optimistically with a smirk.

"Not going to happen. Besides, I don't have authorization."

"Then let me talk to someone who does have authorization," said Wilkens. "My guess is that time is of the essence, for both of us."

"It's already been taken care of," said Hansen. "Cogent Armadillo Solutions, or CAS to you, is fixing your problem."

"You're kidding, right?" asked Wilkens in dismay. He couldn't believe his ears. "You hired a second-tier tech company to fix something that I wasn't able to fix? You must be really desperate or total idiots," said Wilkens with disdain.

"You don't fool me. We all know that CAS is your competitor. That gives them an added incentive to succeed where you failed. Because after they correct your mistake, I suspect they'll be getting many more government contracts."

"I'm not trying to fool anyone. And they're not my competitor. I'm not trying to sell the government anything. Don't you see what's happening here?" asked Wilkens.

"This is what I know, so listen up. You were given access to the government computer system. You had enough time to flush out the virus. You said the operation was successful. Three days later, the computers in the financial systems are down, and the credits have disappeared," said Hansen.

"You think I had something to do with that?" asked Wilkens. "You guys don't know what you're dealing with. You have to let me back in. I need to refine my theory on what's happening, and it's only going to get worse."

"I'll be happy to pass on what you know to CAS. They're the main team taking point now."

"I'm not giving you jack shit until I get a new deal and a restroom," said Wilkens. Sitting was becoming increasingly uncomfortable. He tried crossing his legs and then uncrossing them. Squirming around in his seat didn't help either, the frustration increasing by the minute.

"There is no new deal. All I can offer is leniency if the information you provide pays off. That is if it helps CAS solve this problem. It's only a matter time before they figure it out on their own. Then you'll be back in prison for good," said Hansen with a chuckle. He stood up and signaled for the guard to take Wilkens to the restroom before returning him to the holding cell.

Wilkens stood up for the guard. Checkmate. He felt despair, having nothing left in his game plan. What irked him, even more, was missing his daughter's upcoming recital. Would he ever be able to forgive himself? Would she? If Cogent Armadillo Solutions figured out what was happening and succeeded in solving the problem, Wilkens would lose all leverage to secure his release.

Chapter Five

The new techs rolled equipment into the central control room. The cases bore the company's CAS logo, emblazoned in bright orange and black, Cogent Armadillo Solutions. The company had agreed to a lucrative opportunity to eradicate the bug from the government computer systems once and for all. The head of the company bragged that their lead technician, Dregis, had previously worked for an elite government agency in the high-tech cyber-crimes division.

The President's office had assigned Saul Pendleton, head of the Procurement Division, a leadership role on the Task Force to eradicate the virus from the World Government computer systems. Saul knew that Dregis had worked on some of the same projects as Wilkens.

If Wilkens was unable to clear the bug from the system, Dregis would be the next best person in line to try. They kept the activity logs from the last purge when Wilkens thought he had cleaned the virus from the entire system.

Dregis studied the data and uploaded the pertinent information into the specialized equipment he had designed to deal with situations such as these. Because of the previous company's contract with the government, CAS remained in the shadows of the industry. But this new opportunity would give CAS the platform it needed to make itself indispensable to the World Government and open the lucrative door to other potential clients.

Chapter Six

Clarence Rainer, the Systems Supervisor, observed the assembling of CAS's equipment within the central control room. As CAS neared completion of the task, Dregis, the lead technician, approached Clarence.

"Impressive looking, isn't it?" asked Dregis.

"I'll be impressed if it actually works," said Clarence. He was cautiously optimistic at this point, as Wilkens mistakenly thought he had previously debugged the system. Plus, there was the massive payment deadline looming, just a few short hours away. The impending dread wasn't helping to calm anyone's nerves.

"Although the new equipment has never been field tested on a scale as large as the government computer systems, I am confident it will do the job," said Dregis.

Clarence studied the shiny equipment in front of him. He noticed a bulky harness with multiple wires and sensor pads sprawled on one of the tables. Dregis moved past it and grabbed a sleeker, black sensory input device with one single wire cable. Attached to it was a small pad with what looked like thousands of electrodes.

"Aren't you using this wire harness thingy? What does it do exactly?" asked Clarence.

"We call it the octopus. It's the original prototype and backup of what I'm using now. The agency used it before we developed the new technology. My company redesigned it for improved efficiency."

Dregis turned around to show the back of his neck. He brushed aside his hair to reveal a white square patch that looked like a tattoo at the base of his skull. Dregis peeled the top layer of skin from the patch, to show a black square input node. The plug that Dregis had picked up from the table cleanly snapped on top of the block.

"This is the next-generation neural interface. Much more compact, easy to store, with less material to deal with. And the interface connections at the back of my neck directly communicate with the pertinent areas in the brain. You could say I can directly jack into the system," said Dregis. "We're just about ready to begin. Please take a seat and stay out of my way."

Clarence held his tongue and clenched his jaw. Dregis was clearly in the driver's seat and Clarence was just the passenger. There was nothing he could do but step away as instructed, his eyes not revealing his anger at Dregis' arrogance.

Once everything was set, Dregis fired up the system. There was no monitor screen to see what was going on, but Clarence could tell the system was activated because the equipment control panel suddenly lit up.

"Will we be able to see your progress within the system?" asked Clarence, his voice showing his concern.

"That's a negative. As it is, we had to rush aspects of the equipment to meet your deadline. There wasn't any time to add all the bells and whistles. So, no. You won't be able to see what's happening. But not to worry. I'll report fully on everything I see and do, once the job is completed," said Dregis.

Dregis activated the neural link. Clarence could tell Dregis was jacked in with his mind fully integrated with the system. Dregis' body language showed it all. His limbs tensed up and then relaxed. The chair he sat in kept his body from flopping over. The neck support kept his head upright.

Although Clarence couldn't see his face, he imagined Dregis' eyes were vacant as he focused his mind on viewing the electronic environment of the government computer system.

It was a waiting game now.

Chapter Seven

Several minutes had passed with no significant activity. The techs monitoring the equipment seemed bored and kept quiet. Every so often, they adjusted the settings, but other than that, everyone remained still.

Clarence noticed it right away. He saw a slight twitching of Dregis' left hand. And then the right hand. Then both hands twitched. Fingers undulated like little spider legs trying to run away. Finally, Dregis' body went into a full convulsion lasting for a minute or more before one of the techs screamed out.

"What's wrong with him?" shouted Clarence.

Jonas, the tech in charge of overseeing the operational equipment, looked up from his station, his eyes wide. "I don't know. I've never seen this before."

"Quick, help me release him. Is it safe to shut down the equipment and detach from the system?" asked Clarence.

"I'm not sure whether it's safer to leave him there or take him out," admitted Jonas.

"What's this red emergency button? Is it a panic switch?" asked Clarence.

Without waiting for a response, he hit the big red button. The equipment attached to Dregis' neural interface shut down immediately. The humming of the electronics wound down as the remaining power drained out of the capacitors and circuits. Dregis' body remained still, but slumped. Clarence detected a faint odor of burning flesh, probably cooked brain tissue.

Someone had called for medical assistance. A few moments later, a medic ran into the control room, detached Dregis from the equipment, and checked his vital signs.

"It's too late," said the medic. "He's dead."

Chapter Eight

Wilkens sat in the interrogation room. Déjà Vu. It seemed like the same old drill, but somehow different. Something was up. At least he now knew not to fill up his bladder during these sessions.

"What is it this time? You must have hit a snag," said Wilkens.

"I hate this more than you do. So, cut the arrogant crap," said Switzer.

"I was right, wasn't I? Did CAS screw up? I tried to warn you about them," said Wilkens.

"You can't blame us entirely. You make it extremely difficult to deal with you," said Switzer.

Wilkens sat in silence, contemplating his next move. This was new ground with potential, and he had to play his cards just right.

"The government is prepared to make you a new deal," said Switzer.

"A new deal?" asked Wilkens. He hadn't expected this. "As far as I know, you didn't honor our first deal. I did what was asked, and yet, I still find myself in this hell hole."

"Let's not open up old wounds," said Switzer. "We're running out of time."

"Any new deal we make cannot be rescinded," said Wilkens. "Every time I do work for you, I put myself at risk. I'm not willing to do that again until I know the deal is firm. Whether there's a new threat or not, I eliminate the immediate problem I am tasked with, and you honor the deal. There's no changing the agreement."

The Assistant Attorney General remained quiet for a moment. He knew it was his fault for making Wilkens a better negotiator. He nodded his head. "Agreed."

Chapter Nine

Wilkens examined the preliminary autopsy report. The MRI of Dregis' brain showed dark foci in the areas of the electrodes. Using the team and equipment from Virtual Sentinel Technologies (VST), he analyzed the data from the CAS database. With Victor in charge of the team, Wilkens knew he didn't have to worry about who was watching his back.

"Looks like his brain got fried. I could see that whatever Dregis encountered in the system created an amplified feedback loop which overwhelmed the safety protocols, sending a lethal retrograde current up along the electrodes and into his brain," said Wilkens to Clarence.

Wilkens walked over to the table with CAS equipment. He picked up the octopus and chuckled to himself.

What an ass, thought Clarence, feeling disgusted with Wilkens' attitude. A man just died trying to do the right thing.

Wilkens saw the look of disdain on Clarence's face, but he didn't care. He never got along with Dregis because of his arrogance and how he was always taking shortcuts. During their time working together at the agency, Wilkens had warned Dregis' carelessness would get someone killed. Who knew Dregis would end up responsible for his own death? Was it poetic justice?

It was apparent to Wilkens where CAS had made some ingenious strides in the technology. But they sadly lacked in other areas, mainly safety. It was like jumping out of an airplane with a paper parachute in a storm.

"I see CAS shamelessly copied technology from the agency. I recognize these as prototypes we developed back when we were under contract there."

Wilkens went back through the autopsy report and scanned the pictures. He stopped at an image of the back of Dregis' neck. The picture showed the square patch of electrodes implanted there.

"I see they developed this technology further and bypassed an entire safety layer. So, CAS was able to get the user a direct neural interface with any system they were patched into."

After a few minutes of examining the equipment, Wilkens came up with a working theory. He opened a screen to do some research.

"I need an hour to modify this equipment before I am able to proceed," said Wilkens. He looked over at Clarence who hadn't said a word the entire time.

"Let us know what you need, and I'll make sure you have it," said Clarence. He pulled out his tablet and started texting furiously.

Wilkens had his duffel bag of special equipment delivered prior to his arrival at the central control center. He rummaged through it, searching for something specific. After dumping out half of the bag's contents, Wilkens smiled broadly and pulled out a black zippered pouch. He unzipped the bag and removed a small rectangular device wrapped in cord. He unwound the cord and started soldering the connections to one of the CAS circuit boards.

"What does that do?" asked Clarence. He was further perplexed when he glanced at the screen where Wilkens was doing his research. A word kept cropping up, *Myrmecology*, whatever that was.

"This allows my equipment to talk to the CAS equipment," said Wilkens. "It will also allow external viewers to see what I do once I enter the system. If everything goes well with my upgrade, we should be ready to start in about half an hour."

Chapter Ten

"Tell me what you're doing differently from Dregis," said Clarence.

"For starters, the equipment that Dregis used was drastically deficient in safety protocols and filters. He took needless risks. Part of the software package used was ingenious, but it looks like it was hastily assembled without regard to user safety," said Wilkens. "I'm surprised the government allowed this."

Ignoring Wilkens' disillusionment and obvious attempt at posturing, Clarence continued. "Have you addressed those issues with your upgrades? I mean, you'll be safe, right?"

"Without a proper field test, it's hard to tell. But I addressed what I think are the major failings," said Wilkens. "There's no time to get a neural implant like the one Dregis had, but my modified prototype should do the trick." He held up the octopus and replaced the electrode pads extending from the wires.

A technician brought in another bundle of equipment for Wilkens. He picked up his holo-emitters and set them up on the table beside the CAS equipment. He switched on the emitters and calibrated them while adjusting the controls on the device he attached to the CAS equipment.

A moment later a holo-screen came up and showed a virtual interior of the government computer system. The resolution for these monitors was significantly higher than what Clarence and the others had experienced previously when they believed they had wiped the virus from the system.

"You still haven't told me what you think will be different from what Dregis experienced," said Clarence.

"I've studied the data, I examined Dregis' body and the CAS equipment that he used. I have no wish to meet the same fate as Dregis," said Wilkens disapprovingly. "Of course, I'll be handling things a bit differently than the amateurs. Even though I haven't tackled this specific type of problem before, I am confident. This isn't my first rodeo, you know."

Clarence noted the hubris in Wilkens' words. What was it about these tech guys and their arrogance? But right now, time was running out, and Wilkens was their best option. Clarence could afford to give him a bit of leeway in that respect, especially if Wilkens pulled it off.

Wilkens checked the monitoring equipment and readied his own station for incursion into the government computer system. A commotion broke out at the back of the central control center. It was Saul. He spoke excitedly to Clarence, then scurried over to Wilkens.

"Not so fast. We've added another condition before you can proceed," said Saul.

"Oh, really? I thought time was of the essence. You do want me to stop this virus, right?" said Wilkens. He was astonished by the government's never-ending attempt to meddle in the affairs of professionals.

"The government officials want to ensure you succeed this time. After all, you are getting a full pardon, whether you succeed or not. And for that, we want one of our own guys to assist," said Saul.

The revelation hit everybody in the room like a ton of bricks. The crew was so quiet that only the low humming of electronic equipment could be heard.

"Who would that be?" asked Wilkens with surprise.

Victor stepped forward to volunteer.

"Not Victor," said Saul dismissively.

Wilkens understood the rationale. Victor was a VST employee, not government.

Saul looked over at Clarence, who just stood there stunned. With his thumb pointed toward himself, Clarence mouthed the word, "*Me?*" He was an administrator, definitely not a tech warrior.

Wilkens looked over at Clarence and he eyed him from head to toe, sizing him up. After a momentary pause, Wilkens nodded his head and said, "Agreed."

"Don't I have a say in this?" asked Clarence.

"We don't have much time," said Saul. "You're the best qualified to represent us. You're going in. That's an order."

Clarence's shoulders slumped, and he gave a resigned shake of his head. "Fine. What do you need me to do?" He accepted his fate and prepped mentally for the task at hand.

"Relax Clarence," said Wilkens. "It's a piece of cake. I'll do the heavy lifting. You're just there as an observer. Nothing to worry about."

Wilkens walked over to a rack of surplus equipment and dug around one of the CAS equipment cases. He pulled out another octopus and modified it for the additional incursion station they had to set up. One of the other techs rolled in a chair for Clarence.

"Please have a seat," said Wilkens to Clarence as he gestured toward the chair.

Clarence took the chair as requested. "Will this hurt?" Upon seeing all attention on him as if something bad was going to happen, his heart raced, and he started to hyperventilate.

"Breathe slowly," Wilkens reassured him. "I've got something else for you."

Wilkens helped him strap in and hooked him up with the octopus.

"In order to prepare you to disassociate the physical sensations from your body and to accept the sensory impulses from within the virtual computer system, you're going to need to take this pill." Wilkens held out an off-white transparent gelatin capsule between his fingers. "It's a ketamine derivative. Once ingested, you should feel the effects of the pill within 15 minutes. It will also help you relax. Take it now. By the time we finish setting up, the effects of the pill will have kicked in."

Clarence took the pill as instructed. He followed it with a full glass of water and sat in the chair while the technicians fussed over him, placing electrodes at specific spots on his head and neck. Gradually, Clarence felt his mind disassociate from his body. It was like he was floating in the air. He knew where his arms and legs were, but somehow they seemed like separate entities from his body.

It was nearly impossible to describe. It was something one had to experience. The surroundings gradually faded from his vision and were slowly replaced with a scene within his mind of the virtual computer system. He could still hear Wilkens talking, but it didn't sound like he heard through his ears. The sound appeared to come from a farther distance.

Wilkens took only a moment to strap himself into the chair.

"Don't you have to take the same pill that Clarence took?" asked Saul, his eyebrows furrowed up with an inquisitive look.

"I've done this before, and my brain is trained to set itself in the disassociated mode at will. Therefore, the pill is no longer necessary," said Wilkens proudly. "Yes, my mind and body are conditioned to do this sort of thing. You could say I am the world's foremost expert at it."

The final preparations were made. Wilkens looked over at Clarence. Clarence was already in a world of his own, or more likely already waiting in the virtual computer world.

"Move your left pinky if you're ready to do this," said Wilkens as he continued watching Clarence.

There was a split-second delay, but Wilkens definitely detected movement of Clarence's left pinky. Wilkens nodded and activated his own neural interface.

Chapter Eleven

Wilkens and Clarence stood together in the virtual world at the main hub in awe. It appeared as a huge atrium with a domed ceiling like a wheel with hallways radiating outward in every direction from the center. Their neural interfaces added a whole new dimension to the experience as if they were in another world.

"Where to?" asked Clarence with hesitation.

Wilkens looked at his wrist out of habit, but nothing was there. "Just a minute."

He swiped his hand from left to right in front of him and activated a virtual window. From the pull-down menu, he highlighted and selected an item. Immediately, two protective suits sprouted from thin air and covered them. Built into the suit was a wrist display, but in fact, it was a Virtual Navigation System (VNS). Wilkens studied the VNS and pointed toward one of the hallways. "Follow me," he said and took off at a jog.

Clarence stumbled at first, not accustomed to his virtual legs, but he soon got the knack of it. The corridor was clear of viruses, but as they continued, the number of viruses or blobs increased in numbers. They were able to follow the path just by noting the rising number of viral blobs along the way, without consulting the VNS.

"It's just like following breadcrumbs," said Wilkens.

Clarence nodded in agreement. They stayed on the path until it became wall-to-wall viral blobs. The ground was slick, each step impeded by the blobs everywhere.

"Can we do anything about these little buggers? They're irritating," asked Clarence.

"We can, but it would be fruitless," said Wilkens. "Unless we find the source of these viruses, we'll be wasting our time just picking them off one-by-one or even if we carpet-bombed them. Remember the last time we tried it, they came back with a vengeance."

"Okay," said Clarence. He had momentarily forgotten that experience. They thought they were clear of the bug, but now it had come back in full force. He deferred the matter to the expert, Wilkens.

"Hold on," said Wilkens. He pulled up the virtual screen and punched in a few digits. Two high-powered sniper rifles and two knapsacks full of the dispersion grenades used during their last encounter materialized.

"I took the liberty of programming these beforehand. If it makes you feel better, you can start taking out some of these viral blobs. Even though it's not going to be effective in the long run, doesn't mean we can't have some fun. Besides, I've been waiting for an opportunity to play with these new rifles," said Wilkens.

Clarence shrugged and shouldered one of the knapsacks. He selected a rifle and eagerly examined it. "Thanks for appeasing my sense of security."

"My pleasure," said Wilkens with pride. He smiled and continued taking point.

They took random shots at the viral blobs without stopping. Each time they hit one, it would explode in a burst of red goo. The red goo disintegrated into a darker red dust-like substance and then dissipated into nothing.

Before they reached the epicenter of the infection, Wilkens' VNS beeped. The beeping got louder and increased in frequency as they pressed onward. Wilkens checked the VNS again. This time it was flashing and showed a focal point just ahead of them. He tapped on the flashing dot to bring up all available metrics. "This is what Dregis must have encountered."

"What do you think it is?" asked Clarence.

"Whatever it is, it looks big," said Wilkens. They cautiously approached the main node where the corridor led toward the financial systems. A low vibration and humming permeated the area.

"Do you feel that?" asked Wilkens.

"Yeah, I think we're getting close," said Clarence, trying to sound brave. The waver in his voice betrayed him.

"Not only that but notice the number of viral blobs here," said Wilkens. "We're knee-deep now." It was like wading through the muck in a swamp, each stride making a sucking sound as they lifted their legs for the next step.

Wilkens dug into his knapsack and pulled out a handful of grenades. He pulled the pins and tossed the explosive devices well ahead of them. Both men ducked down beside an embankment for shelter from the blast. The grenades went off and cut a swath of path ahead. Viral goo splattered everywhere before drying up and disappearing.

The men proceeded toward the massive object as detected on the VNS while continuing to clear the path with the grenades. Soon the humming got louder, and a constant distinct rhythm could be detected. As they rounded the corner, they looked up with widened eyes.

In unison, they cried, "Holy shit!"

Chapter Twelve

Clarence and Wilkens couldn't fathom what they were seeing. In front of them was the source of the viral blobs. It was the mother bug, and she towered way over their heads. Wilkens' rendering software depicted the mother of all viruses as a huge mechanized spider-like bug. It pulsed, releasing viral blobs from the end of its abdomen while simultaneously emitting gurgling sounds.

"Look at that mother!" yelled Wilkens.

"It looks like we found BugsE in our system," said Clarence.

"I like that. BugsE, it is. That's her name," said Wilkens.

Suddenly it all made sense to Clarence. The research window Wilkens had opened in the central control room was on Myrmecology, the study of ants. "Do you think she's like a queen ant?"

"That's my theory," answered Wilkens.

"How do we take her down?"

"Your guess is as good as mine."

The two men stood there as BugsE continued spurting out the viral blob babies at a rapid pace.

Chapter Thirteen

The men looked at each other. Wilkens signaled Clarence to follow his lead.

"Let's see what these weapons can do."

They took several grenades, pulled the pins, and tossed them beside the gigantic mother bug. They took cover as the grenades exploded. All around the bug, the red viral blobs splattered. A moment later they had disintegrated into a fine red dust and then disappeared.

BugsE remained. She was clearly agitated and uttered a horrendous screech. The sudden loss of her babies caused an increased production of the viral blobs.

"Well that didn't go as planned," said Clarence.

Wilkens' analytical mind kicked into gear. "Fascinating. There's a positive feedback loop at play. We managed to clear the current blobs, but as long as she's in the system, there will always be more produced."

"How does that information help us?" asked Clarence.

"It doesn't, really. It only reinforces what I've been saying about destroying these viral blobs before we get rid of the source. It's just a waste of time and resources."

"What do you suggest we do?" asked Clarence.

"When we lobbed the grenades at her, she did seem to be momentarily stunned. Albeit a small effect, it did affect her, nevertheless," said Wilkens. "I suggest we get a bit closer to see if we can find any vulnerable areas to exploit."

"I don't like the sounds of that. You go first," said Clarence anxiously.

With a grin and nod, Wilkens moved toward the giant bug. They approached cautiously, allowing for a large buffer zone between them and BugsE. Wilkens lead the way while Clarence remained in the rear. They made sure to stay well back in case BugsE decided to charge or do whatever bugs do.

"You flank her right, and I'll take her left," said Wilkens excitedly. "Keep the channel open on your suit-to-suit communicator. If she makes any sudden moves or does anything unpredictable, fall back to our original position. Got it?"

"Got it," said Clarence. The thought of screwing up worried him.

Wilkens proceeded onward in a huge arc in front of BugsE to avoid being grabbed by her front pincers. He maneuvered over to BugsE's left side. He then spoke into his suit-to-suit communicator.

"Clarence, can you hear me?"

"I can hear you loud and clear," said Clarence. "Go ahead."

"On my signal, lob a couple grenades at BugsE. And then start shooting her with your rifle."

"Roger that. Readying grenades." Clarence shouldered his rifle and took out a handful of grenades from his knapsack. "Give me the count."

"On the count of three," said Wilkens. "One, two, three."

On the final count, both men lobbed their grenades from each side of the beast. Grenades landed in BugsE's proximity. They exploded and destroyed the new viral blobs surrounding the mother. The force of the blast knocked the huge bug over on her side. Then each man fired their rifles into the main body of the creature.

BugsE writhed and screeched in agony, the legs on her right side bearing the brunt of her weight. Clarence, feeling more confident after watching the bug fall to her side, advanced closer. He kept firing, concentrating on BugsE's midsection.

"Watch yourself. Don't get too close," warned Wilkens.

But Clarence remained focused on his one task, no longer terrified. The adrenaline coursing through his blood gave him overwhelming courage. In a split-second, the bug righted herself.

"Look out!" screamed Wilkens.

Too late. The bug's prehensile forelegs snagged Clarence and pulled him into her waiting pincers. Surprised and without time to think, Wilkens ran up and under the beast. He fired furiously overhead into the creature's underbelly. From that vantage point, he saw a faint greenish light pulsating beneath BugsE's exterior armor. As Clarence thrashed about in fear within the creature's pincers, he kicked the armor plate and loosened it.

Wilkens realized what he was seeing. It was the creature's kill switch, except this one was protected by armor plating. Clarence had kicked it loose, but it still stayed in a protective position. The bug snapped its pincers shut, virtually cutting Clarence in half. He screamed in agony as an energy spike traversed along his neural interface and fried his brain. His body went limp.

"No!" yelled Wilkens.

In a renewed fight for survival, Wilkens tried to maneuver under the bug for a better vantage point to access the armored panel. But it was out of his reach. Then he felt his body leave the ground as BugsE grabbed him by the legs. With his upper body still free, he grabbed a grenade and pulled the pin.

But now the bug had a firm hold on him. He grasped onto the other legs so that the bug could not get his body into its pincers. He found he was right up close to the underbelly of the creature. The armor panel covering the kill switch came into view. He was close. In a swift, angry motion, Wilkens forced his hand with the grenade under the loose armor panel. He let the grenade go and anxiously pulled his hand back out. The armor plate stayed in place, trapping the grenade within.

Wilkins released his grip on BugsE's legs, allowing the creature to pull Wilkins' body up toward her pincers. He would meet the same fate as Clarence. But before the bug could chomp on him, the grenade detonated. Wilkens felt BugsE shudder with the explosion. He was thrown back several meters, the bug's disembodied prehensile appendages still grasping onto his legs.

The beast had blown up, scattering mechanized pieces and bug goo all over before disintegrating into dust and disappearing.

-To be continued in Book 3-

If you enjoyed this title, I would appreciate your leaving a review of the book. Good reviews encourage an author to write as well as help books to sell. Good reviews can be just a few short sentences describing what you liked about the book without having a spoiler. If you could spend 30 seconds writing a review, I would appreciate it: you can review this title right now at your favorite retailer.

Here is a preview of the **next story** you may enjoy:

THE COCKROACH scuttled silently along the baseboard and up to the sink. It cautiously explored the toothbrush with its undulating feelers. Satisfied with its destination, it lay a sticky, viscous transparent egg-like mass within the bristles.

After finishing its task, the critter crawled back down the sink and disappeared behind the baseboard. Within the walls, hidden away from prying eyes, the cockroach convulsed and rolled on its back, legs up. A tiny plume of smoke emerged from its thorax as an enzyme pouch erupted from within. In mere moments, the cockroach body disintegrated into a desiccated exoskeleton.

The alarm went off at the usual time of 4:30 AM. Before the second alarm cycle had a chance to sound off, a hand slapped down on the bedside clock, thus ending its morning rant.

The man made a slight groan before sitting up and rubbing his face to clear his eyes. Sliding into his slippers, he stood and shuffled into the bathroom. The face looking back from the mirror showed lines of weariness, cut deep from too many difficult decisions made over the years.

Turning on the faucet and applying some toothpaste, he brushed his teeth as he had done so many mornings before. Except that this time, something was different. A sharp pain emanated from the left side of his chest. The intense pain exploded unnaturally fast. He stumbled to the floor and was dead before his head hit the porcelain rim of the toilet.

<<◇>>

Tyler Wilkens had just settled into his window seat on a full flight. He was flying on the shuttle to make it home in time to attend his daughter's recital. Since being released from prison, he was determined to become more involved in her life. And that included participating in her extracurricular activities.

His daughter, Sterling, showed exceptional promise with the viola and she was so excited when Wilkens told her on the video call that he was attending her performance. But something nagged at Wilkens from within his core. His unhindered freedom seemed too good to be true, and he tried to force it from his mind before it became a self-fulfilling prophecy.

Although he had succeeded in eradicating the virus from the World Government's computer system, the win had come too late and at great cost. The World Government missed a crucial debt payment to OmniClon Universal (OCU) and now had to face substantial penalties. The specter of Clarence's death also weighed heavily on his shoulders. Clarence Rainer, the Systems Supervisor, was an administrator, not a fighter. The government bureaucrats had insisted that Clarence accompany Wilkens on his mission despite the risks.

None of those things was Wilkens' fault, but the ominous feeling he was experiencing came to a head.

Three black sedans, with lights flashing and sirens blaring, rushed onto the tarmac and blocked the plane from approaching the runway.

After what seemed like hours, four agents, dressed in black suits and sunglasses, boarded the plane. The lead agent spoke to one of the flight attendants. She pointed down the aisle, and all eyes fell on Wilkens.

Here we go again. Wilkens slumped down in his seat, trying to look small. The disappointed look on his daughter's face flashed through his mind, and it broke his heart. He hoped she would forgive him. He knew what was coming next.

If you enjoyed this sample then look for **Coup D'etat: The Cyber Heist Files - Book 3**.

Other Books by Freddie Kim

- The Time Guardian Thriller Series

- Stinger Jacked

Get the latest update on new releases from the author at:

https://www.freddiekim.com/newsletter/

About the Author - Freddie Kim

As a child, Freddie Kim would make blanket forts and refrigerator-box space ships, both essential things needed to repel against invasion from an alien race. Freddie has never really grown up from his childhood fantasies. The inspiration that he draws from the memories of his youth is captured and revealed to all in his writing.

Connect with Freddie Kim

I really appreciate you reading my book! Here are my social media coordinates:

Friend me on Facebook:
https://www.facebook.com/FreddieKimAuthor/

Follow me on Twitter:
https://twitter.com/freddiekimauth1

Check me out on Goodreads:
https://www.goodreads.com/author/show/16961603.Freddie_Kim

Subscribe to my newsletter:
https://www.freddiekim.com/newsletter/

Visit my website: https://www.freddiekim.com/